Charlie—cute, funny-face cat lover.

First printed in Great Britain in 2008 by Penguin Books Ltd.

ISBN 978-1-338-32540-9

12 11 10 9 8 7 6 5 4 3 2 1   18 19 20 21 22 23

Printed in the U.S.A.   40

First Scholastic printing, September 2018

A Forest Charm

SUE BENTLEY

Illustrated by Angela Swan

SCHOLASTIC INC.

Prologue

The young, silver-gray wolf padded through the trees. Patches of snow still lay on the hillside, gleaming in the spring sunlight. Storm lifted his head. It felt good to breathe the cold air of his home.

Suddenly, a terrifying howl rang out.

"Shadow!" Storm gasped. The fierce lone wolf who had attacked the Moon-claw pack and wounded Storm's mother was very close.

There was a flash of bright golden light and a shower of dazzling sparks. Where the young wolf had been standing, there now crouched a tiny puppy with fluffy white fur, a stocky body, and short legs.

Storm whined with terror and his little puppy heart beat fast. He hoped this disguise would protect him from his enemy.

His puppy paws kicked up the soft snow as he tore through the trees. There was a steep ridge ahead of him. Perhaps there would be somewhere to hide. Storm glimpsed a tangle of tree roots that had formed a natural cave and headed toward them.

As he approached, Storm saw wolf eyes gleaming from within the darkness of the roots. He caught his breath and skidded to a halt, ready to turn and run away as fast as he could.

"Storm! In here, quickly!" the wolf called out in a soft growl.

"Mother." Storm sighed with relief. He rushed forward and pushed through the tangled roots until he reached the she-wolf.

"It is good to see you again, my son," Canista rumbled, licking her disguised cub's fluffy white fur and little square muzzle.

Storm yipped a greeting. He wriggled his body and wagged his stumpy tail as he licked his mother's face. "I have come back to lead the Moon-claw pack!"

Canista's gentle eyes lit up with pride. "Bravely said, but now is not the time. Shadow wants to be leader and he is too strong for you. He has already killed your father and litter brothers and left me weak from his poisoned bite."

Storm curled his lip in a growl, showing small sharp teeth. He knew that his mother was right, but he was reluctant to leave her.

"The other wolves will not follow Shadow—they are waiting for you. Go back to the other world. Use this disguise. Return when you are stronger and wiser, and then face Shadow." As Canista finished speaking, she gave a wince of pain.

Storm huffed out a shimmering gold puppy breath, which swirled around his mother's wounded paw and then disappeared into her gray fur.

Canista narrowed her eyes. "Thank you. The pain is easing."

Another fierce howl rang out, sounding much closer.

"Shadow knows you are here. Go. Save yourself!" Canista urged.

Bright gold sparks bloomed in the tiny puppy's downy, white fur. Storm whimpered as he felt the power building inside him. The gold light around him grew brighter. And brighter . . .

Chapter
ONE

Cassie Yorke stamped moodily through the forest in her new walking boots. She was with her mom and dad and about twenty other adults and kids.

"Why do we have to do this stupid family team-building thing, anyway?" she complained.

Mrs. Yorke gave her daughter a patient smile. "That's the third time you've asked me that since leaving home, Cassie. Your dad's new boss likes to encourage his staff to get along well with one another. And

that includes their families. This weekend
is a way of us working as a team and
getting to know one another better," she
explained.

"But we're going to be camping. How
can that be a challenge?" Cassie asked.

"Ever tried camping without a tent to sleep in, a stove to cook on, and no water on tap?" her dad asked.

"No way!" Cassie said, horrified.

Her mom laughed. "We are supposed to have fun, too. Now try and lose the long face, Cass. Okay?"

Cassie sighed heavily and felt her shoulders drooping to match her face. Traipsing through a cold, muddy forest on a Friday afternoon was definitely *not* her idea of fun! She had been planning to curl up by the log fire in the living room and finish reading her book. *Lost in the Amazon* was the latest in the series about the amazing adventures of ace explorer Jilly Atkins.

Her dad came over and put his arm

around her shoulder. "Come on, Cass.
Where's your spirit of adventure? Just
try and imagine you're Jilly Atkins!" he
suggested cheerily.

"As if!" Cassie said.

Jilly was tall, strong, brave, and fearless.
Not small and dumpy like Cassie felt,
and she had probably never been teased
for being a slowpoke when doing school
sports.

"Here we are now," Mrs. Yorke said
as the group came in sight of a large,
wooden cabin with a sign above the door
that read *Wild Wood Experiences*.

After the welcome and introductions,
two instructors divided the group into
teams: the Reds, Blues, and Greens. Cassie
and her mom and dad were in the Reds.

"Oh great. We've been teamed up with Ronson from the office. He's a real know-it-all," Mr. Yorke said softly.

Cassie saw a fit-looking man who towered over her dad. Mr. Ronson was tanned and broad-shouldered and looked as if he practically lived at the gym. His wife and daughter were both thin and dark-haired.

"Well, we're supposed to be getting to know one another better. Should we go over and say hello?" Cassie said.

Mr. Yorke gave her a mournful look. Despite herself, Cassie couldn't help smiling.

As the adults exchanged greetings, Cassie went over to Mr. Ronson's daughter. "Hi, I'm Cassie."

"I'm Erin," the girl said, tossing her long, silky hair over her shoulder.

Cassie looked at her enviously. She

wished her hair would grow that long, but her blond curls just seemed to grow outward and get bushier.

Erin didn't really say much. Cassie thought she might be shy, so she made a special attempt to be friendly. "I'm dreading this. I've never been even normal camping or anything. Have you?" she asked, smiling.

Erin shrugged. "No, but I've done tons of outdoor stuff with my dad. This is going to be easy-peasy. But how come *you're* here? The rules say you have to be at least ten before you can participate."

"I'm almost eleven actually," Cassie said, her smile wavering.

"But you're so small! I thought you were only about eight," Erin said rudely, looking Cassie up and down.

"My gran says good things always come in small packages," Cassie shot back. She was used to people making comments about her size and usually found that making a joke of it got over any awkwardness.

But Erin didn't even grin. "Yeah, well, your gran would have to say that, I guess. I just hope you're not going to hold our team back. My dad only plays to win. He always says that you don't get any prizes for coming in second."

Good for him, Cassie thought, starting to feel annoyed. "My dad's motto is 'It's the effort that counts.' I like that one much better!"

"Huh!" Erin gave Cassie a pitying

look before skipping over to stand with her mom.

Mrs. Yorke noticed her daughter's annoyed face. "Are you okay, Cassie? You're not still sulking, are you?"

"Of course not. I'm fine now," Cassie said, putting on her best fake smile.

After meeting Erin, Cassie wished more than ever that she could be at home with her head in her book. There didn't seem much chance of the two of them making friends this weekend.

Before the teams set off into the forest, the instructors gathered them all together again for a few words about health and safety. Cassie's tummy suddenly growled, making everyone laugh.

It had been a long drive to get there

and lunch seemed like hours ago. Cassie felt more than ready for a snack. There were some chips and chocolate in her backpack, but she hesitated about getting them out. Erin was looking her way and she didn't want to hear any more sarcastic comments.

As people stood around chatting outside

the cabin, Cassie saw a chance to slip away. "Just heading to the bathroom!" she called to her dad.

"Okay, honey. Don't be long," he said.

Cassie headed past the bathroom and ducked around the back of the cabin. She was alone with just the open forest in front of her. Fishing in her backpack, she pulled out a bar of chocolate.

"Yum, yum," Cassie breathed, licking her lips.

She was about to take a big, luxurious bite, when suddenly, a dazzling bright flash of gold light shot out in all directions from the bush in front of her.

Cassie blinked hard, blinded for a moment. She rubbed her eyes and saw a tiny, cute puppy with fuzzy, white fur, a stocky body, and short legs crawling out of the bush.

"Can you help me, please?" it woofed.

Chapter
TWO

Cassie gaped at the little, white puppy in utter amazement and the chocolate bar slipped from her numb fingers on to the ground.

She must be so hungry that she was hearing things! Talking puppies didn't just appear to small and ordinary girls. Even Jilly Atkins had never met one and she'd explored all kinds of strange and remote places.

Cassie shook her head, laughing at herself. Her dad always said that she had an overactive imagination.

"Hello, you," she crooned, rubbing her fingers together to encourage the tiny puppy to come closer. "I think you must be a little Westie. Aren't you gorgeous? I wonder which of the instructors you belong to."

The puppy pricked its ears, and two bright, midnight blue eyes looked up at her from behind a little fringe of fluffy, white fur. "I belong to no one but myself. I am Storm of the Moon-claw pack."

Cassie did a double take. She snatched her hand back as if it had been burned. "Y-you really c-can talk?" she gasped.

"Yes, I can. Who are you?" the puppy yapped.

Cassie still couldn't quite believe this

was happening, but she didn't want
to scare the amazing puppy away. She
squatted down to make herself seem
smaller and less threatening.

The puppy pricked its ears and put its
little head to one side, waiting for her to

answer. Although Storm was really tiny, he seemed quite sure of himself.

"I'm Cassie. Cassie Yorke. I'm here with my dad to do some family team building. It's part of Dad's new job," she explained.

Storm bent his neck in a formal bow. "I am honored to meet you, Cassie." He took a few steps closer and reached out his neck.

Cassie grinned delightedly as the cute puppy's buttonlike black nose twitched and then she felt the little wet tip brushing against her fingers. She gently rubbed Storm's soft chest and then moved up to stroke his ears.

It still felt really weird to be having a conversation with a puppy, but Cassie's

curiosity began to take over from
her initial shock. "We're miles from
anywhere in the middle of this forest.
How come you're here if you don't
belong to anyone?" she asked, puzzled.

Storm's tiny body began trembling
all over like a leaf. "An evil lone wolf
named Shadow is looking for me. He
killed my father and litter brothers and
injured my mother. Shadow wants to
lead the Moon-claw pack, but the others
will not follow him while I live."

"But you're just a helpless little puppy.
Why would an evil wolf—" Cassie began.

Storm backed away. "I will show
you!"

There was another flash of bright gold
light, and big sparks rained down all

around Cassie and sizzled on the damp
forest floor as they landed.

"Oh!" Cassie cried, blinking hard.
But as her sight cleared, she caught her
breath.

The tiny, white puppy had disappeared
and in its place there crouched a majestic,
young, silver-gray wolf with bright
midnight blue eyes. Specks of gold dust

gleamed in its fur and shone from within its deep neck-ruff.

Cassie eyed the wolf's sharp teeth and powerful muscles. "Storm?" she breathed nervously.

"Yes, it is me. Do not be afraid. I will not harm you," Storm told her in a deep, velvety growl.

While Cassie was still struggling to take in the sight of Storm as his magnificent real self, there was a final dazzling flash and Storm reappeared once more as a tiny, white, scared-looking West Highland terrier puppy.

"Wow! That's an amazing disguise!" Cassie said, completely overwhelmed by what had just happened. "Shadow will never recognize you now."

Storm blinked up at Cassie with a troubled expression. "Shadow will use his magic to find me as soon as he can and then no disguise will protect me. I need to hide now. Can you help me?"

Cassie's soft heart went out to the terrified little puppy. With his bright blue eyes peeking out from behind his bangs, square little face, and pointed ears, he was the most adorable thing she had ever seen. "I'd really love to. But I don't see how I can," she said, chewing her lip. "We have to take part in lots of awful exercises. I bet some of the families might think a puppy would slow us down too much." Cassie frowned as she thought about the Ronsons in particular.

"Do not worry, Cassie!" Storm barked

softly, jumping up and pawing her
waterproof pants. "I will use my magic
so that only you can see and hear me!"

"You mean—you can make yourself
invisible? Cool! Then you can come

with me. Maybe you should do it now before someone sees you."

Storm shook himself, so that tiny sparks flew out of his fluffy, white fur. "It is done."

"Yay! It's going to be fantastic having someone nice I can talk to this weekend," Cassie said. "Wait until I tell Dad about you. He's great at keeping secrets!"

"No! Only you must know I am here. You can never tell anyone. Promise me, Cassie," Storm woofed, his little face serious.

Cassie felt disappointed that she couldn't even tell her dad the exciting news. But Storm looked so scared, gazing up at her with pleading, blue eyes. Cassie

decided then and there that if it would
help to keep Storm safe, she was prepared
to agree.

"Okay. Cross my heart! That's my own
way of saying I promise," she said as
Storm's furry, white brow wrinkled in a
puzzled frown.

"I've been looking everywhere
for you!" an irritated voice suddenly
demanded from behind her.

Cassie froze as she recognized Erin's
bossy tone.

"Who on earth are you talking to?"

Chapter
THREE

Cassie whipped around guiltily. "Me?
I was just talking to . . . er . . . myself,"
she said hastily.

"Your dad sent me to find you," Erin
grumbled. "I thought you said that you'd
be in the girls' bathroom."

"Um . . . yeah. I've just . . . er . . .
finished in there," Cassie said distractedly.
"I forgot the way back."

Storm was sitting there large as life
barely a foot away. Even though Storm
had said he was now invisible, Cassie

couldn't quite believe it. She tensed,
waiting for Erin to notice the little
puppy. But the older girl didn't comment
and Cassie began to relax.

"I'm coming now," she said, reaching for her backpack.

"About time, too," Erin scolded.

Storm was now rolling on his back in the grass. He looked as cute as could be with his fat, pale tummy showing and all four of his short, white legs in the air. Cassie had to try really hard not to giggle.

"What's so funny?" Erin asked sounding annoyed.

"Nothing," she said, forcing herself to concentrate. Luckily, Storm stood up and shook himself just as an extra-big giggle rose up in her chest. Cassie hastily turned it into a cough. "Sorry . . . er . . . frog in my throat. I bet it's going to take forever to make a fire and build a shelter and stuff," she said, quickly changing the subject.

Erin smirked. "Not with *my* dad helping, it won't! Mom says he's a whiz with power tools. He can make anything. He made me an amazing tree house, with a ladder and slide and everything."

I'd like to see him try to plug in an electric screwdriver in the middle of the forest, Cassie thought, fed up with Erin's boasting.

"Hey!" Erin cried, spotting the chocolate bar on the ground. She swooped down and picked it up. "Is that yours? Have you been eating a secret snack?"

"No, I have not!" Cassie said truthfully. Well, it was true that she hadn't eaten any chocolate—yet. And after finding

Storm, she'd forgotten all about it.
"Anyway, so what? It's only one tiny
little bar."

"It's against the rules to bring your
own food. Let's see what the others have
to say when I show them this!" Erin
waved the bar in the air triumphantly.

"Give it back!" Cassie cried, jumping
up to try and reach it, but Erin kept
dodging out of her way.

Suddenly, Storm streaked upward,
shedding a glittering rocket's trail of gold
sparkles behind him. He shot between
Cassie and Erin, grasping the bar in his
sharp little teeth. Tossing his head, he
pulled the chocolate out of Erin's hand.

"What—" Erin looked up in surprise at
her empty hand.

Storm drifted to the ground in another flurry of sparks. Laying back his ears, he bounded away into the bushes.

Cassie bit back another grin. Because Erin couldn't see Storm, she must have

thought the chocolate had tried to escape by leaping into the air all by itself!

"I don't get it. Where did that chocolate go?" Erin said, frowning.

"Beats me," Cassie said casually. She didn't even mind losing the chocolate bar. It was worth it to see the look on Erin's bratty face! Cassie slung her backpack over her shoulder. "What are you waiting for? I thought we were in a hurry."

Still looking puzzled, Erin began following Cassie.

Storm exploded out of the bushes in a flurry of leaves and came tearing over to Cassie with a wide, mischievous grin on his little, square, white face.

"Thanks, Storm. You were fantastic. I
don't think Erin will bother telling on me
now that the evidence has disappeared!"
she whispered.

"I am glad I was able to help," Storm
woofed. He stretched and then kicked
at the ground with his short, back legs,
sending a tiny spray of muddy grass in
Erin's direction.

Erin skirted sideways to avoid getting spattered. "There are some megafreaky breezes in this forest," she commented.

Cassie thought she was going to burst with laughter. Clapping both hands over her mouth, she broke into a jog. Having Storm as her own special teammate this weekend was going to be the most fun ever.

Chapter
FOUR

Cassie's spirits were high as the group trekked along a forest track. Storm was trotting along beside her. Her earlier annoyance at Erin's unfriendliness faded into the background as she thought about her amazing new puppy friend. The morning flew by and it seemed like about five minutes before they all reached a clearing.

Storm's ears twitched as he looked up at the tall, sweet chestnut trees that surrounded the area. There were lots of fallen branches, and a thick layer of gold and orange leaves covered everything.

"This is a safe place," he woofed.

Cassie quickly checked that no one was listening before answering. "I'm glad you like it. Because it looks like we're about to set up camp here," she whispered.

The instructors explained that the Reds,

Blues, and Greens would need to make everything they needed from materials they could find around them. There would also be a special task for the kids from each team.

"I wonder what that's going to be," Cassie whispered to Storm.

He sat at Cassie's feet, all attention. His fluffy, white bottom was parked on her walking boots. She had to stop herself from bending down to stroke him.

"This suddenly seems like an awful lot of hard work," her dad said. "I hope we don't actually have to hunt for our food as well." His face was red and sweating from the walk. Cassie could see there were damp patches on his T-shirt through his open shirt.

She gave him a little nudge. "Think of it as a challenge, Dad! The Red team rules, okay!"

He scrunched up his face, but then reached across to ruffle her mop of fair curls. "Well, I'm glad to see that you've perked up. I thought our most difficult task was going to be cheer-up-the-grumpy-daughter!" he teased.

"Da-ad! I wasn't that bad. Was I, Mom?" Cassie said, grinning.

Mrs. Yorke smiled and held up her open hands. "I'm saying nothing!"

Everyone had a drink of bottled water before they started work. Cassie took a swig of hers and then bent down and pretended to be fiddling with her boots. Making sure that no one was watching, she poured some water into her hand for Storm.

His soft, whiskery little muzzle tickled her as he lapped it up. "Thank you, Cassie," he woofed, licking his chops.

"There'll be a prize for the team who constructs the best shelter and another for the one that gets a fire started. You might find it helpful to elect a leader," an instructor was explaining.

Cassie's attention was still on Storm when Mr. Ronson's loud voice suddenly made her jump.

"I'll be the Red team's leader," he boomed. "I'm the most experienced at outdoor skills. Any objections?" he asked.

"Er . . . well . . ." Mr. Yorke murmured, looking a bit stunned.

"No? That's settled then," Mr. Ronson said.

After the Blue and Green teams had decided on their leaders, an instructor explained about the kids' task. "While the adults build a shelter to sleep in, you're going to look for a hidden package,

containing fire-making tools. There's one for each team. And there'll be a prize for the team who gets their fire going first."

"That sounds like fun," Cassie whispered to Storm. "And you'll be able to have a good run around the forest."

Storm nodded and eagerly wagged his stumpy tail.

As the teams moved apart and then set to work, Mr. Ronson took charge. "Okay. You two can start by collecting some branches. We need to trim them before we use them to build the shelter," he said, jabbing a finger at Cassie's mom and dad, before turning to his wife. "And you can collect some twigs for firewood. Okay, guys, get to it!" he ordered.

Cassie's dad made a wry face at her

before he set off toward some fallen branches.

"I see what dad means about Mr. Ronson. He's really enjoying bossing everyone around, isn't he? No wonder Erin's so unbearable," Cassie said to Storm.

Storm growled very softly in agreement.

Cassie suddenly noticed that Erin was looking at her with narrowed eyes and angry, flushed cheeks. She realized that she must have spoken more loudly than she'd intended to and Erin had heard her.

She chewed at her lip, feeling guilty. No one liked to hear someone else criticizing their dad. "Erin, I'm really—" Cassie was about to apologize, but just then Mr. Ronson came over.

"Okay, you two. You need to find that hidden package and get back here with it pronto. That prize for lighting a fire first is ours, okay?"

"No problem. I won't let you down, Dad," Erin said.

"Don't you mean *we* won't let the *team* down?" Cassie asked.

Erin ignored her. "Does Cassie have to come with me? She'll only lag behind and slow me down!"

Cassie saw Storm's fuzzy, white fringe dip in a frown. "That is not a very nice thing to say!" he yapped.

Cassie agreed with him. "But I wasn't very nice about her dad, though, was I? Erin's probably just getting back at me," she whispered to him.

But Storm snorted and didn't seem so sure.

"The task is for both of you. Those are the rules, Erin," Mr. Ronson said. He handed Erin a small map and a piece of chalk. "Why don't you show Cassie how it's done by setting a good example?"

"If I have to," Erin said reluctantly, slanting a sideways look at Cassie. "But it won't be my fault if she messes up."

Mr. Ronson patted his daughter's arm. He smiled down at Cassie. "I'm sure you'll do your best, dear. A team's only as strong as its weakest member, you know."

Charming, Cassie fumed quietly, but wisely chose not to say anything.

Erin began studying the map as her dad

walked back to the rest of the Reds.

"Can I have a look?" Cassie asked, going toward her and peering over her shoulder.

After they had both worked out the

way to go, Erin crumpled up the map and threw it on the floor.

"Erin!" Cassie cried, angry at the older girl's littering. But before she could go and pick the map up, she saw Erin already stomping off through the trees.

"Well, come on!" Erin called back impatiently.

Cassie sighed and she and Storm set off after her. She decided she would pick the map up on their way back.

At first Erin walked at a normal speed, swinging her arms, but the moment they had left the campsite she broke into a run, tearing away from Cassie and Storm.

"Hey! Hang on!" Cassie called to her, speeding up.

Erin looked over her shoulder and

wagged her fingers in a wave. "Come on, slowpoke!"

Cassie gritted her teeth in determination and broke into a run. She pumped her arms and legs like crazy as she tried to catch up with long-legged Erin. But it was no use. Erin easily outpaced her and was soon out of sight.

Cassie slowed down and then stopped in frustration. "Oh fudge! Forget it! I've always been terrible at running," she puffed. "Erin's just going to get the package by herself and then brag about it to everyone. Maybe she was right about me being useless. I should have stayed behind at the camp."

"That is not true, Cassie. I will help you catch up to her," Storm woofed.

Suddenly, Cassie felt a strange tingling sensation flowing down her back as bright gold sparks began igniting in Storm's fluffy, white fur, and his pointed, white ears crackled with electricity.

Something very strange was about to happen!

Chapter
FIVE

Cassie watched in amazement as Storm lifted one little white paw and sent a fountain of gold sparks whooshing toward her. They swirled around, whirling faster and faster and then began forming into the shape of a magnificent horse with a dazzling white coat and a flowing gold mane and tail.

The next instant, Cassie found herself seated on the back of the beautiful horse. "Wow!" she breathed, patting its warm, silky neck. "This is amazing!"

Storm leaped up in front of her in another little flurry of sparks and Cassie wrapped her hands in the thick golden mane and held on tight. The horse snorted and pawed the ground with one elegant hoof, before it galloped away in a blur of speed. Storm's fluffy, white fur rippled in the breeze as they raced along, searching for Erin.

Cassie laughed with delight as trees flashed past them. Now and then the horse veered expertly to one side to avoid a particularly big tree, or wove through the tall bushes.

"I feel just like Jilly Atkins in *Outback Trail*," she told Storm.

"Is Jilly one of your friends?" Storm barked.

"No. She's not a real person. She's a character in books and computer games. But I like her because she's strong and brave and she always tries to do her best."

Storm turned to look up at her. "Just like you!"

Cassie smiled at him. No one had ever

called her strong and brave before. "Look, there's Erin!" she cried, pointing at a thin figure standing beneath a spreading oak tree. "Good job, Storm!"

Once again, Cassie felt a prickling sensation down her spine. There was a flash of golden sparkles. The horse melted into a wisp of white and gold smoke before disappearing with a soft *Pop!*, and then she and Storm were standing on the leaf-covered ground behind a thick bush.

Cassie started hurrying toward Erin, with Storm trotting invisibly beside her. She pretended to be out of breath as if she'd been running hard.

Erin turned around as Cassie came lumbering up to her. "Oh, it's you," she said, scowling.

"Thanks very much for waiting for me," Cassie said sarcastically.

"Well, you should have got a move on. I can't help it if you're a slowpoke," Erin scoffed.

Cassie felt her temper rise as Erin hit a raw nerve. "Don't call me that!" she exclaimed in frustration. "It was your fault I couldn't keep up. You deliberately ran off and left me!"

"Okay. Relax," Erin said warily, taking a step back. "Maybe I was a bit too excited to get going. Anyway, you're here now, aren't you? Look. That's where the package must be hidden." She pointed up into the branches where a red flag was fluttering from a fork in the trunk. "One of us has to climb up and get it."

Cassie could see that the flag was fairly high up, but the trunk had plenty of knobbly spots for safe hand and footholds. She paused, expecting Erin to leap forward and scale the tree in her usual "me-first" way.

But Erin looked unusually tense. "Go ahead. What are you waiting for? Climb up there, Cassie!"

But Cassie was fed up with being bossed around. "Why don't we flip for it? Loser climbs up." She took a quarter out of her pocket, tossed it and covered the coin with her hand. "Your call."

"Heads!" Erin said.

Cassie uncovered the coin. "It's tails. You lose."

"How about best of three?" Erin said quickly.

Cassie shrugged. She tossed the coin twice more and won each time. "Congratulations! You go up the tree."

The color drained from Erin's face.

She hung her head. "I . . . er . . . can't," she murmured.

Cassie frowned. "Why not? It's an easy climb."

"I don't like heights, okay?" Erin snapped. "I guess you think I'm pathetic now, don't you?"

Cassie was shocked. The way Erin had behaved so far, she didn't think the older girl would be afraid of anything. She was tempted to tease Erin now and get her back, but seeing how nervous Erin looked, she decided not to.

"No, I don't think you're pathetic," Cassie replied. "It's no big deal. Everyone's scared of something. I'm scared of big, hairy spiders."

Erin looked relieved. "You won't tell

anyone, will you? Dad doesn't believe in being scared of things. He says everyone has to face their fears. That's what he always does."

"Yeah, well not everybody's that strong," Cassie said. "Of course I won't say anything."

"Thanks," Erin said, smiling with genuine warmth for the first time since Cassie had met her. She looked much softer and prettier without the scowl she wore so often.

Cassie found herself wondering for the first time whether she and Erin could become friends. It would be really nice as their dads worked together and they'd probably get to meet each other again in the future.

Cassie took a firm handhold on the oak's trunk and then braced her foot against a ridge of bark. She swung herself up, climbed up to the fork, and reached for the package.

From her high vantage point, she smiled as she caught a glimpse of a small white shape diving into a bush. Storm was obviously chasing a poor rabbit again!

Cassie climbed down carefully. She had barely reached the ground before Erin grabbed the package out of her hands and tore it open. A small key-ring-like object, but with only two small, metal tags, fell into her hands.

"The flint and striker. Now we can go back and get a fire started," Erin said triumphantly. "I really want to win that prize. Let's go!"

Cassie followed as Erin set off confidently. But they had only been walking for a couple of minutes when Erin stopped and looked around. "I'm not sure which way to go now."

"Me neither. I can't see any chalk marks on the trees—" Cassie stopped as she saw the look on Erin's face.

"I forgot to make any," Erin murmured, looking a bit embarassed.

And Cassie knew why. Erin had been too intent on leaving her behind to mark a chalk trail back to camp.

Erin's face fell. "We're completely lost. What are we going to do?"

Chapter
SIX

Cassie knew that Storm would easily
be able to follow their scent trail back to
camp, but he was busy chasing rabbits.
With Erin so close, Cassie couldn't call
him. She knew that Storm was bound to
come and find her soon, but of course
she couldn't tell Erin that.

Cassie tried to think of some way
of causing a delay. As she shifted her
backpack, she heard a faint crackling of
chip wrappers.

"I think I'll have a quick snack before

we start off again," she said, playing for time. She sat down and took out a bag of chips. "Do you want some?"

Erin looked at her in disbelief. "No, I don't! Don't you care that we're lost? How can you just sit there stuffing your face?"

"Easily," Cassie said, munching happily. "Chill out, Erin. Something will turn up; it always does."

Erin stamped her feet. "We're going to be *so* late back. I know my dad's counting on winning both prizes. He'll be furious that he can't start the fire."

"I thought you said he was an expert at outdoor stuff. Can't he rub two sticks together or something?" Cassie suggested reasonably.

"Don't be stupid. That would take forever!" Erin snapped. "Okay! I'm going to try and find my way back now. You can stay here if you'd like. See if I care."

"Will you just hang on for thirty seconds? I'm thinking," Cassie said.

"Yeah, I can hear the rusty wheels

going around," Erin sneered.

"Ha-ha," Cassie said, thinking that Erin's new friendliness hadn't lasted very long.

Just then, Storm emerged from the bushes. He came running over with his tongue lolling out and jumped into Cassie's lap. Bits of twig and leaves speckled his white fur. "I had a very good time. Are we ready to go back now?" he panted.

Cassie pretended to be zipping up her backpack, so that she could whisper to him. "Yes, but Erin didn't put chalk marks on the trees, so we don't know which way to go. Can you find the way for us, please?"

Storm jumped to the ground, his

stumpy tail wagging. "I will be glad to
do that!"

"Great." Cassie jumped to her feet and
dusted herself off. "I think those chips
must have fed my brain because I can
remember the way back now," she said,
winking at Storm. "Follow me, Erin!"

Erin shook her head slowly as Cassie

stomped off. "You are so annoying, Cassie Yorke!" she cried.

"That makes two of us then," Cassie said cheerfully.

As Cassie, Storm, and Erin walked back into camp, they saw that all three teams were finishing their tents. The Blues and Greens had fires blazing in front of theirs.

Cassie's mom called to her as she approached. "Everything all right, sweetie?"

"Fine. We found the package," Cassie replied, smiling.

"Good job," her mom said warmly.

Mr. Ronson frowned at Erin. "All the other kids got back a long time ago.

What happened? I expected better from
you, Erin."

Erin hung her head. "I'm sorry . . . I
didn't . . ." she began hesitantly.

Cassie felt sorry for her. It couldn't be
much fun having such a strict dad. "It
was my fault. I forgot to put any chalk
marks on the trees, so we got lost," she
interrupted quickly. "Erin was great,
though. We were wandering around
forever, but she somehow found the way
back here."

Mrs. Ronson put her arm around her
daughter. "Did you? Good job, Erin."

Erin threw Cassie a grateful look and
gave her a rather shaky smile as she
handed the flint and striker to her dad.
"Well, at least we can get the fire started

now. Better late than never, I guess," Mr. Ronson sighed.

"That was a good thing to do. You are a kind human, Cassie," Storm woofed.

"Thanks, Storm. But I think even Erin deserves to be rescued from such a bossy dad!" she whispered to him, smiling.

Cassie and Storm went to see how their tent was coming along. It had a square frame made of branches lashed together. More branches leaning against it formed a slanting, open-fronted shelter. Inside it, a thick layer of dried leaves made a soft surface to sleep on.

"It looks quite cozy in there now, doesn't it?" Cassie said.

Storm seemed to agree. He immediately bounded into the shelter and began nosing around. Leaves flew in all directions as he scuffed them up with his front paws.

"Careful. Someone might notice all this stuff being stirred up by itself," Cassie gently reminded him.

Storm put his head to one side, grinning apologetically. "I am sorry, Cassie. There are so many interesting smells here. I am enjoying exploring and rooting into everything."

"Well, that's what puppies do, don't they?" Cassie said fondly.

Storm nodded happily and suddenly dashed off toward an interesting-looking tree stump.

Cassie hid a grin as she watched him. She felt a surge of affection for her cute, mischievous friend.

Later, Cassie secretly shared her meal of canned beans and sausages with him. The light began to fade as they were clearing away and the moon rose over the trees. An owl hooted as Cassie was spreading out her sleeping bag.

Erin came over to put hers next to Cassie. "Thanks for what you said to my dad about it being your fault that we got lost," she said quietly as they both got ready for bed.

"That's okay," Cassie said, pleasantly surprised. "Good night, Erin."

"G'night, Cassie. Sweet dreams," Erin said sleepily.

Cassie snuggled down with Storm's little warm body next to her. The air was soon filled with soft snores, but she lay awake, enjoying looking out of the open-fronted shelter. The sky was deep purple and blazing with silver stars, like a million tiny diamonds. She wondered whether Storm could see the same stars in his own world.

Cassie felt a deep glow of happiness. "I love having you here. I hope that you can stay with me forever," she whispered to him.

Storm twisted his head to look at her, his midnight blue eyes glowing brightly in the moonlight. "That is not possible. One day I must go back to my home world to face Shadow and lead the Moon-claw pack. Do you understand that, Cassie?" he woofed, his little, square, white face serious.

Cassie nodded sadly but she didn't want to think about that now. This moment was just perfect as it was. She kissed the top of Storm's fluffy, white head. "Sweet dreams," she yawned as she drifted off to sleep.

Chapter
SEVEN

It was cold and misty when Cassie woke the following morning. No one else was awake. She lay snuggled up inside her sleeping bag for a while longer, cuddling Storm's warm, stocky, little body.

"This is nice and cozy, isn't it?" she whispered, stroking his fluffy fur.

Storm looked up at her and she saw his midnight blue eyes darken with sadness. "Yes. It is like being curled up in a safe den with . . . with . . ." he woofed and then trailed off into a deep sigh.

He's thinking of his mother and the Moon-claw pack in his own world, Cassie realized with a pang.

There must be something she could do to help him feel better. "I know! How about an early morning walk?" she suggested.

Storm pricked his ears, and his face brightened a little. "I would like that!" He sprang out of the sleeping bag and wagged his stumpy, white tail.

The others were starting to wake up now. Cassie quickly dressed and pulled on her boots. "I'll grab some water for washing," she called, picking up a bucket.

As she and Storm went off in the direction of the nearby stream, hazy bars of sunlight pushed through the mist hanging over the trees. There was a smoky smell of frosty autumn leaves in the air.

Storm tore around as usual, scrabbling under fallen logs and sniffing at clumps of grass. He ran toward Cassie with a broken branch in his mouth and dropped it at

her feet. Crouching down on to his front
paws, he barked hopefully.

Cassie laughed and threw the branch
for him to fetch. With a happy bark,
Storm ran after it. He seemed to be
feeling much happier than when he woke
up—just as Cassie hoped he would.

She swung her arms as she walked,
feeling perfectly happy. At the stream,
she kneeled down to fill the bucket
from a spring gushing down over some
rocks. Storm was splashing around in the
shallows a few feet away.

He jumped out onto the bank and
came lolloping up to Cassie. His white
fur stuck up in little wet peaks and there
was a mischievous expression on his
dripping face.

"Don't you dare—" Cassie began, but it was too late.

Storm's whole body shivered from head to foot as he shook himself. A shower of droplets splashed all over Cassie.

"Storm! You little terror! You did that on purpose!" she scolded laughingly. "It's a good thing I'm wearing waterproof clothes."

Storm beamed and stood up on his short back legs to paw at her pants. His sharp puppy teeth were very white against his little black lips.

As they made their way back to camp, the delicious smell of frying bacon floated toward them.

"I like human food," Storm yapped hungrily.

Cassie's mouth watered, too. Why did food always smell so much better outdoors?

"Hello, sweetie. You're an early bird this morning," Mrs. Yorke said as she turned bacon in the pan.

Mr. Yorke was just opening a can of tomatoes.

"Hiya, parents," Cassie sang out as she

put down the bucket of water. Storm's cheerfulness was infectious. "I was wide awake, so I thought I'd do something useful."

Her dad goggled his eyes. "Quick, someone, call the police! Someone's stolen our Cassie and swopped her for this helpful, strangely cheerful girl!" he joked.

"Da-ad!" Cassie pretended to swipe him on the head.

She wished she could tell them that the reason why she was so happy was sitting there invisibly, wagging his little white tail. Cassie would have loved to see the looks on their faces, but she knew that she would never give away Storm's secret.

That afternoon there were team games. The most fun was when each person took turns being blindfolded, and then their teammates talked them through an obstacle course.

"I will make myself glow very brightly and you will be able to see me through the band around your eyes. You can just follow me," Storm woofed, eager to take part.

"No. That would be cheating. I have to do this myself, but thanks, anyway," Cassie told him.

So instead, Storm joined in by padding around on tiptoe behind the person wearing the blindfold. Cassie laughed so much that others began to laugh, too, and even Erin joined in.

"I didn't think this game was *that* funny!" Erin said, giggling and wiping her eyes.

"It's not!" Cassie spluttered.

Later there was more firewood to collect and then a short talk about identifying and collecting wild food. Time passed quickly for Cassie and soon, after dinner, everyone sat around in a circle to do a task together.

"You can make everything you need from the materials around you. We're going to make some cord from a plant you can find growing almost anywhere," the instructor said, producing a bundle of green stems.

"Ouch! Stinging nettles!" Cassie said nervously.

Storm twitched one ear. After having rushed around all day, he was lying next to her with his nose resting on his paws.

"Hold your nettle like this," said the instructor, holding the stalks at an angle. "Now, push firmly upward to strip off the leaves. Try it. You won't get stung if you do it like this."

"It would be much easier if we all wore gloves," Mr. Yorke joked.

Cassie grinned at him.

"Gloves?" Mr. Ronson scoffed, obviously taking her dad seriously. "I suppose you'll want a cushion to sit on next! Come on, man. Rise to the challenge!" He pushed up his sweatshirt sleeves, flexed his bulging muscles, and then began rubbing his palms together noisily.

As her dad's face reddened, Cassie tingled with embarrassment on his behalf.

She couldn't stand the way Erin's dad always had to show off.

"Me first!" she shouted on impulse. Gritting her teeth, she leaned forward and grabbed a big, hairy nettle, exactly as the instructor had shown her. It didn't sting at all. She ran her hands upward toward the top and the leaves fell off on to the grass.

"Ta-da!" Cassie crowed, waving the stripped stem in the air.

Mr. Ronson looked at her in surprise. "Not bad," he said.

Coming from him, that was praise indeed, Cassie thought.

As everyone got to work stripping

nettles, the instructor showed Cassie the
next stages in making cord.

Cassie felt a tiny tingle down her
spine. Next to her, little gold sparks were
starting to glisten in Storm's white fur.

She suddenly found herself smoothing, flattening, rolling, and twisting, her nimble fingers flying. In half a minute, she had her first ever piece of strong, green cord. "Storm. I can do this by myself," she scolded gently.

Storm nodded. The sparks in his fur went out. He gave a contented sigh and began dozing as Cassie carried on making nettle cord by herself.

"Are you sure you haven't done this before? You're a natural," the instructor said as the pile of cord in front of her grew.

"I've always loved making things. I guess it's some consolation for being terrible at sports and stuff," Cassie said modestly.

The instructor smiled. "A good team needs 'doers' and 'makers.' It's all about sharing skills."

Cassie hadn't thought of it like that before. She felt a stir of pride. Perhaps being part of a team was something she could be good at after all.

On the other side of the circle, Erin grinned encouragingly.

Chapter
EIGHT

Later that evening, the instructors left
for the cabin, intending to return early
the following morning.

"You should all be fine by yourselves
for a few hours. But we're not far away
and we'll leave you a cell phone in case
of emergencies," one of them said.

"I'll hold on to that phone," Mr.
Ronson said promptly, tucking it into his
pocket.

It was another clear night. Trees cast
long shadows in the moonlight as the

Blues, Greens, and Reds prepared for bed.

Cassie settled down with Storm. "It's Sunday tomorrow. We go home after lunch. You're going to love it there," she told him.

Storm gave a tiny woof and yawned sleepily. He turned around and around in circles before settling comfortably with his head resting beneath Cassie's chin.

Cassie said her good nights to everyone and instantly fell asleep.

She woke suddenly a few hours later, in the dark gray light of dawn. There was a loud drumming noise all around her. At first Cassie couldn't understand what the noise was and then a cold raindrop splashed onto her nose.

She crawled to the open front of the shelter and peered out. Rain was coming down in torrents through the trees. In the semi-darkness, she could just see wriggly lines of water trickling past the shelter. A huge puddle glistened across what had been grass the night before and reached almost to the Greens' tent.

Storm stood up and shook himself.

Lifting his nose, he sniffed the air. "There is too much water. We could be in danger," he yapped, flattening his ears.

"You mean floods? I'd better wake everyone up!" Cassie leaped up and scrambled into her clothes. She leaned over to shake Erin, who was nearest, and then woke both sets of parents. "Quick! There's water everywhere!" she told them.

"It's just a bit of rain, for goodness' sake." Mr. Ronson's voice was muffled from deep within his sleeping bag. "Stop fussing and go back to sleep."

Storm lifted his lip in a soft growl and danced sideways, barking in annoyance. Cassie felt like doing the same thing.

"No! We have to move. Storm says

so!" she burst out, hardly realizing what she'd said. Luckily, no one seemed to have heard her properly.

"What's that about a storm, Cass?" her dad asked sleepily, opening one eye. His hair was all sticking up. "Are you sure you didn't just have a bad dream?"

"I'm not imagining this. Please, Dad, just take a look outside," Cassie said desperately.

"Okay. Anything for a bit of peace," Mr. Yorke groaned.

Suddenly, Erin cried out. "There's water coming in. Ugh! My sleeping bag's getting soaked!"

Mr. Yorke sat bolt upright. "Yikes! Cassie's right. If we don't move soon, we'll be sitting in the middle of a lake!"

Look, the Greens and Blues are already getting up!"

After that, there was a mad scramble to get dressed into raincoats and roll up the sleeping bags. Cassie picked Storm up and cradled him in her arms, keeping him dry beneath her baggy anorak.

As they all splashed across to join up with the other families, the instructors' cell phone rang. Mr. Ronson answered it.

Cassie and Erin were closest to him and both heard some of what he said. "No, there's no need for you to do that. It's not that bad here. Yes, I'm absolutely certain. We can make it back by ourselves," Mr. Ronson said confidently. "Okay. I'll explain to the others. No problem. Leave it to me."

Cassie frowned in puzzlement. Something didn't seem quite right about the conversation. "I wonder what's going on. What isn't there any need for the instructors to do?" she whispered to Storm.

Mr. Ronson began speaking. "We've

been told to make our way back to the cabin. There's a short cut across a bridge, just over that ridge. I went and checked it out yesterday afternoon," he explained.

"That seems a roundabout way to go, when we could go via the track we came in on," Mr. Yorke commented.

Mr. Ronson shrugged. "That may be. But this is the *Wild Wood Experiences* way and the sooner we get moving, the sooner we'll be back. Hurry up now; this way, everyone," he said, waving one arm in a big arc.

"He'll be shouting 'Wagons roll!' in a minute, like in those awful old cowboy films!" Cassie grumbled.

Her dad laughed. "Remind me to buy him a sheriff's badge sometime."

Cassie tramped along, feeling happy
that they were all safe, despite the rain
dripping from her anorak hood. Storm's
little body was warm against her chest
and she could smell his faint, clean puppy
scent. "Are you okay in there?" she
whispered, looking down at him.

Storm reached up and licked her chin.
"I am fine."

The rain slowed and then stopped
as they trudged along. After about
ten minutes, they reached the top of
the ridge. The ground sloped steeply
downward on the other side. At the
bottom, Cassie could see the ditch with
the wooden footbridge over it.

Suddenly, she heard fierce growling
and barking through the trees. Cassie felt

Storm stiffen and begin to tremble all over. "What's wrong?" she asked softly.

"I think Shadow is close. He will have used his magic to make any dogs that are nearby into my enemies. Now he has set them on to me," Storm whimpered softly, rolling his eyes in terror.

"Those dogs do sound like they're getting closer," Cassie said worriedly. "How will I be able to tell if they're coming for you?"

Storm whimpered and Cassie could feel his heart beating wildly. "They will have fierce, pale eyes and extra-long teeth."

The sound of growling was even louder. Cassie felt a leap of fear. Storm was in terrible danger! She racked her brains as she tried to think of some way of protecting the tiny puppy.

A memory stirred within her. In one of her favorite books, Jilly Atkins had been tracked by a hungry bear and had escaped by rubbing something very nasty all over herself to disguise her scent.

"That's it!" Cassie burst out. Without a second thought, she pretended to lose her balance and fall over. "Oh," she cried

as she skidded for real and both legs shot from beneath her.

She landed on her backside with a teeth-rattling jolt. Gathering speed, Cassie went sliding downward in a slippery, muddy avalanche of half-rotten leaves.

Chapter
NINE

Taking care to cradle Storm in both hands, Cassie twisted sideways and began rolling over and over down the slope. She wanted to make sure that she was covered in smelly stuff from head to foot.

As Cassie tumbled to the bottom, she found herself heading toward a big clump of brambles, but couldn't put out her hands to stop herself. Sharp thorns tore at her clothes and made deep scratches in her skin, but Cassie hardly noticed them.

Tearing herself free, she scrambled to

her feet. A strong earthy smell rose up around her.

"Perfect! No enemy dogs will be able to smell you through this stuff."

"Thank you, Cassie," Storm whined

softly. "That was very brave. You could have been badly hurt."

"I couldn't bear anything to happen to you," Cassie said. "Oh," she gasped as the scratches started throbbing now that the excitement was over.

"You *are* hurt! I will make you better," Storm yapped.

Cassie felt a familiar prickling down her spine as Storm huffed out a glittery puppy breath. The softly gleaming cloud floated into the air and then sprinkled down onto Cassie like Christmas glitter. As the golden dust dissolved into her muddy clothes, she felt the soreness fading and all the rips and tears mended themselves instantly.

"Thanks, Storm," she said, stroking his

little warm ears. "I think you'd better stay inside my anorak until we're completely sure that those fierce dogs have gone."

The fear was starting to fade from Storm's deep blue eyes, but he nodded. "I think so, too."

"Cassie!" her mom shouted in a panicky voice, hurtling down the slope ahead of the others. "Are you hurt?"

"No. I'm just a bit shaken up," Cassie replied.

"Thank goodness for that. I can't believe you escaped without even a scratch or the tiniest rip in your clothes. You're a very lucky girl!"

"I know," Cassie said. *I'm the luckiest girl in the whole world—I've got Storm for a friend*, she thought.

Cassie's mom wrinkled her nose. "But just look at the state of you! Phew! You smell awful!"

"I don't mind," Cassie said happily.

"You're going to need a shower when we get back to the cabin," her dad said

when he saw her. "You're so clumsy! Falling down that slope. It's the sort of thing I usually do!" he said.

Cassie realized that he was about to give her a comforting hug, despite the smelly mud. "No, don't, Dad! You'll get all stinky, too," she said quickly, backing away. If he squeezed her, he'd be sure to feel Storm's sturdy little body beneath her anorak.

Mr. Ronson came stamping over. "For goodness' sake! Can't that girl do anything right? Of all the useless—"

"Don't, Dad! Cassie's okay," Erin cried from just behind him. "And it's not her fault, anyway. We didn't have to come this way, did we?"

Cassie's jaw dropped in astonishment.

Did Erin just stick up for her?

"What does Erin mean?" asked Mr.
Yorke.

Mr. Ronson looked rather uncomfortable
as the others gazed at him inquiringly.

A light seemed to go on in Cassie's
head as she remembered the cell phone
conversation. It was starting to make sense
now. "You weren't told to bring us back
this way, were you? That was all your
own idea!"

"Is this true, Ronson?" asked one of
the other dads.

Mr. Ronson nodded slowly. "They
were going to send a van to pick us up
and told us to meet it at the track. But I
told them not to bother. We came here
for the challenge, didn't we? I thought

you'd all welcome the chance of getting back on our own."

"But you didn't bother to ask us if we agreed with you, did you?" Mr. Yorke said angrily. "As a team member, you're the worst. Not to mention that Cassie could have been badly hurt when she tumbled down that muddy slope!"

"But I'm fine, Dad!" Cassie protested.

"That's not the point." Her dad squared his shoulders and stood his ground in front of the taller man. "What do you have to say, Ronson?"

Mr. Ronson shifted his feet. "Okay. I admit that I was wrong. I'm sorry, everyone." He turned to Cassie. "And I'm truly sorry that you almost got hurt. I'll call the cabin right now and tell them to send the van for us after all."

"You do that!" Mr. Yorke said. He looked at Cassie and her mom. "Let's walk around this ridge and make our way to the track."

Everyone else began following as the Yorkes set off. Cassie hung back to thank Erin, but the older girl avoided her eyes and linked arms with her dad.

Cassie sighed as she went to catch up with her mom and dad. "I thought Erin might feel like walking back together, but she doesn't seem to want anything to do with me," she whispered disappointedly to Storm.

"Maybe she just needs more time," Storm woofed wisely. "It could not have been easy for her to stand up to her father."

Cassie nodded. "That's true." She hoped that Storm was right about Erin needing more time, but she was starting to think that they would never be friends.

Chapter
TEN

To Cassie's immense relief, there was
no more growling or barking as she and
Storm made their way to the track, along
with the others.

"I think this smelly mud has done the
trick. Shadow's dogs must have gone
past," Cassie said.

Storm nodded, his midnight blue eyes
thoughtful. "Your plan has worked for
the moment. But I sense that those dogs
are not too far away. If they return, I
may have to leave suddenly."

Cassie felt a pang as she realized that she didn't feel ready to let her magical little friend go. She loved being with Storm so much.

"I'm looking forward to getting warm," she said, deliberately changing

the subject. "And I want a megasized mug of hot chocolate and a mountain of cookies, so I can share them with you!"

Storm perked up and licked his little chops. "That sounds good!"

A big minibus was waiting on the track. The group all piled inside. Cassie lifted the bottom of her anorak, so that Storm could crawl out. She sat with him on her lap, stroking his fluffy, white fur.

Back at the cabin, everyone began changing into dry clothes. With so many people inside, it was pretty cramped. There were wet boots, backpacks, and raincoats everywhere.

"Come on, young lady. Let's get you straight into the shower," said Cassie's mom. "Here you are. You can change into these." She thrust a bundle of dry clothes into her arms.

Cassie went into the large washroom. She soaped and scrubbed herself, enjoying the hot water. Steam filled the shower cubicle, so that Cassie didn't notice Storm press himself into the corner by the door and then keep looking around nervously.

After Cassie finished drying herself, she pulled on her jeans and T-shirt and dry sneakers.

Just as Cassie and Storm came out of the shower, Cassie almost bumped into Erin, who was bent over with her head under a wall-mounted dryer.

"Hi," Cassie said.

Erin stood up and flicked her damp hair back. "Hi."

119

Cassie chewed her lip, trying to think of something to say. "I'm . . . er . . ." she began.

"No, let me go first," Erin said. She took a deep breath and then out it all came in a rush. "I don't suppose you'd . . . er . . . want to come to my house sometime, would you? I know I've been a brat and my dad can be a bit strict and bossy, but he's okay when you get to know him better. And I've just got this amazing new computer game with Jilly Atkins in it and I thought we could— what?" she asked, as Cassie stood there openmouthed.

"I can't believe it. You like Jilly Atkins?" Cassie said delightedly.

Erin nodded. "I absolutely love her.

I've read all her books, except the new one."

"Me too! I'm reading the new one now. You can borrow it after me, if you want," Cassie said, smiling all over her face.

Erin beamed back at her. "Cool! So
you'll get your dad to bring you over?"

"I'd love to!" Cassie said.

This weekend had turned out really
well after all. Cassie had to admit that the
team building had worked well—at least
for her and Erin.

She was still taking these amazing
developments in, when Storm suddenly
gave a sharp whine of terror and shot
toward the washroom door. At that
moment, someone came in and Storm
bolted straight out of the gap.

Cassie's tummy clenched. Storm's
enemies must have come back. He was
in terrible danger. Leaping forward, she
ran after Storm. "Back in a minute," she
called to a puzzled-looking Erin.

Cassie pounded down the hallway. Right at the end of it, she saw Storm's stocky, little, white form dash around a door with *Storeroom* written on it. From somewhere just outside, she could hear loud snarls and growls.

As Cassie reached the storeroom, a dazzling flash of bright gold light streamed out of it. Nervous about what might happen, she slowly opened the door more widely and went inside.

There was Storm, a tiny, helpless puppy no longer, but his true majestic self: a beautiful young silver-gray wolf with glowing midnight blue eyes. An older wolf with a gentle face, whom Cassie guessed was his mother, stood next to him.

And then Cassie knew that Storm was leaving for good. She was going to have to be very brave. She rushed over and Storm allowed her to hug him one last time.

"I'll never forget you, Storm," Cassie said, her voice breaking as she buried her face in his thick, soft fur.

"You have been a good friend. I will remember you, too," Storm said in a deep, velvety growl.

Cassie took a step back just as an ugly growl sounded right outside the door. "Go. Save yourself, Storm!" she urged, her heart aching.

There was a final burst of brilliant gold light and a bright shower of sparks floated down all around Cassie and crackled on the storeroom floor. Storm and his mother faded and then were gone. The growl was abruptly cut off and silence fell.

Cassie felt her throat sting with tears. She was going to miss Storm so much, but at least she knew he was safe.

And she would always have her secret memories of the wonderful adventure they'd shared.

"Cassie? Where are you?" called Erin's voice from the hallway.

"Coming!" Cassie called, heading for the door. She took a deep breath and silently wished magic puppy Storm and his Moon-claw pack well as, smiling, she went to find her new friend for some adventures of their own.

About the Author

Sue Bentley's books for children often
include animals or fairies. She lives in
Northampton and enjoys reading, going
to the movies, and sitting watching the
frogs and newts in her garden pond. If she
hadn't been a writer, she would probably
have been a skydiver or a brain surgeon.
The main reason she writes is that she
can drink pots and pots of tea while she's
typing. She has met and owned many
cats and dogs and each one has brought a
special kind of magic to her life.